A Frog He Would
A-Wooing Go

Grolier Educational Corporation

A Frog he would a-wooing go,

      Heigho, says Rowley!

Whether his Mother would let him or no.

      With a rowley-powley, gammon and spinach,

      Heigho, says Anthony Rowley!

So off he set with his opera-hat,

Heigho, says ROWLEY!

And on his way he met with a Rat.

With a rowley-powley, gammon and spinach,

Heigho, says ANTHONY ROWLEY!

4

"Pray, Mr. Rat, will you go with me,"

    Heigho, says Rowley!

"Pretty Miss Mousey for to see?"

    With a rowley-powley, gammon and spinach,

    Heigho, says Anthony Rowley!

5

Now they soon arrived at Mousey's Hall,

Heigho, says ROWLEY!

And gave a loud knock, and gave a loud call.

With a rowley-powley, gammon and spinach,

Heigho, says ANTHONY ROWLEY!

"Pray, Miss Mousey, are you within?"

Heigho, says Rowley!

"Oh, yes, kind Sirs, I'm sitting to spin."

With a rowley-powley, gammon and spinach,
Heigho, says ANTHONY ROWLEY!

"Pray, Miss M<small>OUSE</small>, will you give us ginger beer?"

Heigho, says R<small>OWLEY</small>!

"For Froggy and I are fond of good cheer."

With a rowley-powley, gammon and spinach,

Heigho, says ANTHONY ROWLEY!

"Pray, Mr. FROG, will you give us a song?"
Heigho, says ROWLEY!
"But let it be something that's not very long."
With a rowley-powley, gammon and spinach,
Heigho, says ANTHONY ROWLEY!

"Indeed, Miss Mouse," replied Mr. Frog,

Heigho, says Rowley!

"A cold has made me as hoarse as a Hog."

With a rowley-powley, gammon and spinach,

Heigho, says Anthony Rowley!

"Since you have caught cold," Miss Mousey said,
Heigho, says Rowley!
"I'll sing you a song that I have just made."
With a rowley-powley, gammon and spinach,
Heigho, says Anthony Rowley!

But while they were all thus a merry-making,

Heigho, says ROWLEY!

A Cat and her Kittens came tumbling in.

With a rowley-powley, gammon and spinach,

Heigho, says ANTHONY ROWLEY!

The Cat she seized the Rat by the crown;

Heigho, says ROWLEY!

The Kittens they pulled the little Mouse down.

With a rowley-powley, gammon and spinach,

Heigho, says ANTHONY ROWLEY!

This put Mr. FROG in a terrible fright;

Heigho, says ROWLEY!

He took up his hat, and he wished them good night.

With a rowley-powley, gammon and spinach,

Heigho, says ANTHONY ROWLEY!

But as Froggy was crossing a silvery brook,

> *Heigho, says* ROWLEY!

A lily-white Duck came and gobbled him up.

> *With a rowley-powley, gammon and spinach,*
>
> *Heigho, says* ANTHONY ROWLEY!

So there was an end of one, two, and three,
Heigho, says ROWLEY!
The Rat, the Mouse, and the little Frog-gee!
With a rowley-powley, gammon and spinach,
Heigho, says ANTHONY ROWLEY!

Copyright © 1988 New Orchard Editions.
ISBN 0-7172-9020-4
Printed in Portugal

E Caldecott, Randolph
C

A Frog he would
a-wooing go